This book belongs to

_____

_____

To my latest addition, Ben,
with love,
Daddy

First published in 2010 in Great Britain by
Gullane Children's Books

© 2010 by Mark Marshall

This 2010 edition published by Sandy Creek,
by arrangement with Gullane Children's Books.

Sandy Creek
122 Fifth Avenue
New York, NY 10011

ISBN: 978-1-4351-2274-1

Printed and bound in China

1   3   5   7   9   10   8   6   4   2

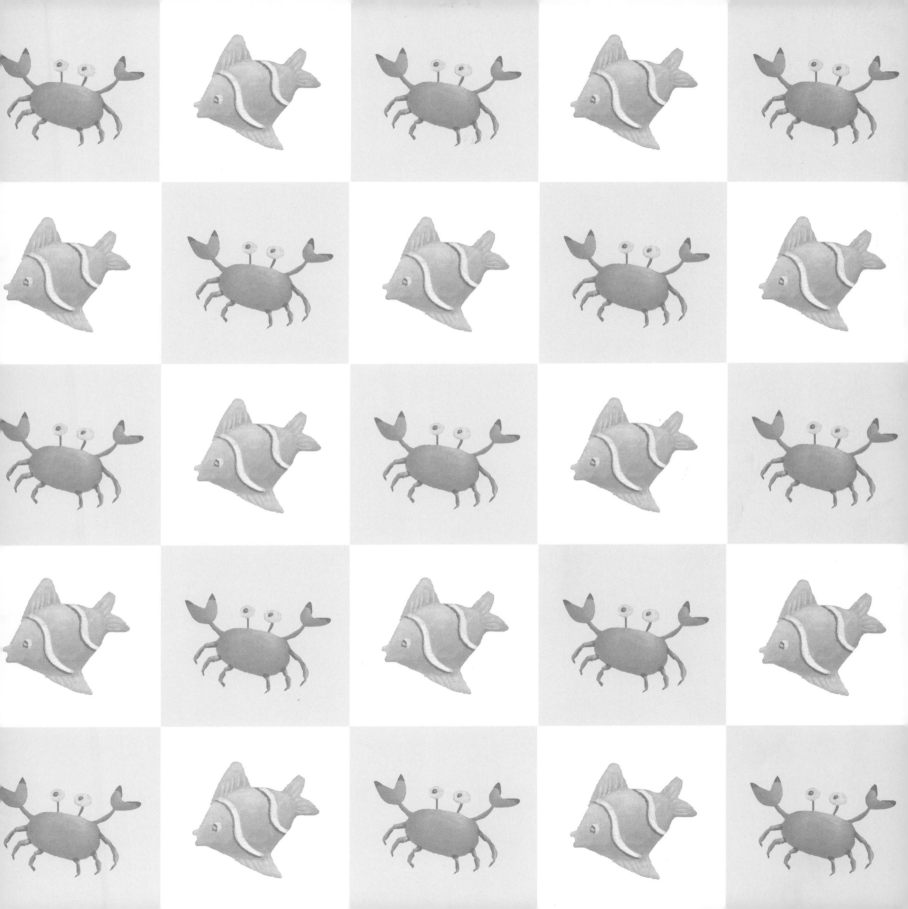

Little Tiger's Big Trip

Mark Marshall

Sandy Creek

My name is Little Tiger
and I need to pack my suitcase,
because with my very best friend Zebra
we're going on a trip.

But what on earth will I take..?

We might fly on a plane,
loop-the-loop through the skies.
Then I'll need some special goggles
so no dirt gets in my eyes.

And if we're very lucky
we might zoom into space.
Floating so high above the earth,
I'll need a rope around my waist.

I'm sure I'll need a snorkel
and some flippers too,
as we dive into the ocean waves
and surprise the fish there - boo!

We may just skydive.
Then as we drift towards the ground,
I'll need a big bright parachute
to keep me safe and sound.

I'm sure I'll need some stilts
to walk high up in the sky.
With so many amazing sights and sounds,
we can watch them all go by.

We might just race each other.
Then I'll need a special hat.
Broom broom zoom, va-va-va-va-voom,
we'll be leaders of the pack!

And if it gets too hot
we can run into the sea,
with Wally Whale and Zebra.
How much fun that will be!

Out on the peaceful water,
there'll be a boat for us to row.
I'll be sure to need some paddles,
but will they fit? I just don't know...

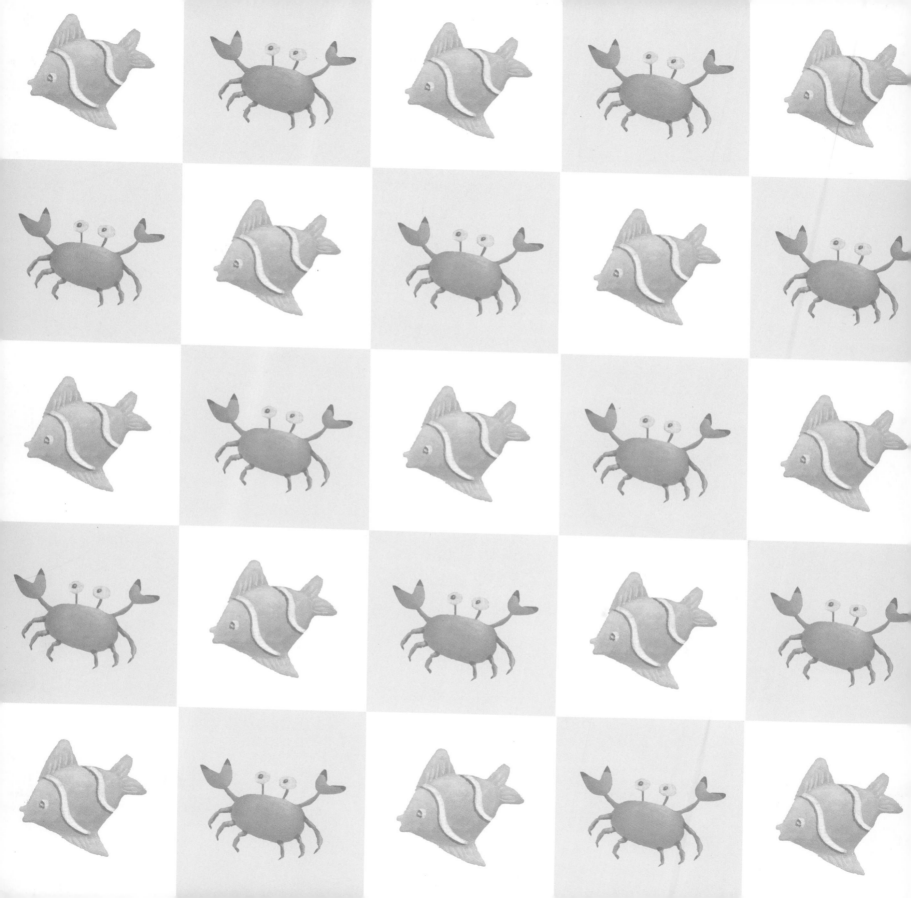